A CURIOUS ROBOT ON MARS!

To IA, with whom I could never be lonely. —JDS

I'd like to dedicate this book to the person who made it all possible: Isabel Atherton. —BS

A CURIOUS ROBOT ON MARS!

WRITTEN BY James Duffett-Smith ILLUSTRATED BY Bethany Straker

Sky Pony Press
New York

Over 100 million miles from home,
the curious robot was all alone.

He loved digging, and
he loved exploring.

But Mars was cold, and Mars was empty.

"CURIOSITY, THIS IS MISSION CONTROL. YOU'VE FOUND ICE, AND YOU'VE FOUND ROCKS. YOUR MISSION IS OVER."

"Mission Control, don't leave me here! There's more to do . . . Hello? . . . Can you hear me?"

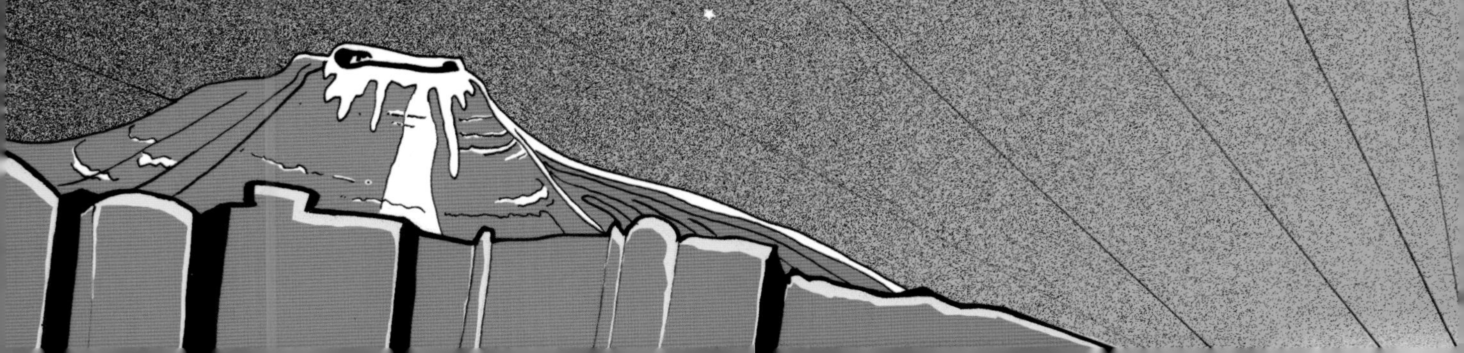

But they couldn't hear him.

Curiosity, the robot rover,

was all alone.

But Curiosity hadn't finished exploring.
He crawled over the red sand and reached
a big crack in a rock.

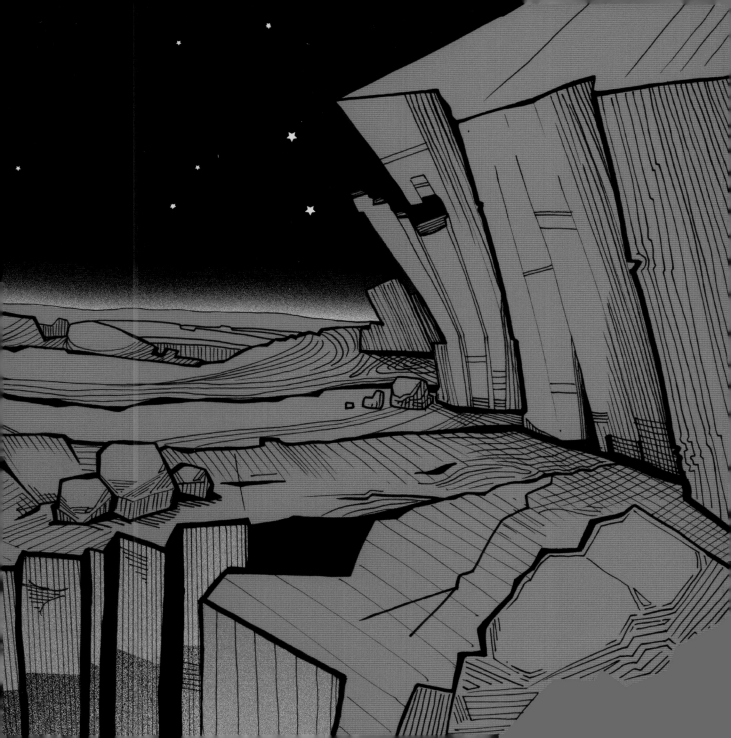

He saw a flash of light at
the bottom of the deep,
dark crack.
"Hello?" he called. "Is
there anybody there?"

Curiosity got too close to the
edge, though, and fell into
the darkness. "Help!" he
cried as he tumbled down.

Curiosity landed at the bottom in a big, soft pile of leaves. The light shone through the crack above.

Out of the light, Laika, the space dog, barked at him. "Rufff! Ruff!"
And next to her Sputnik beeped. "Beeeeeep! Beeeep!"

The light grew stronger at the bottom of the crevice.

Curiosity knew that his mission was now over.

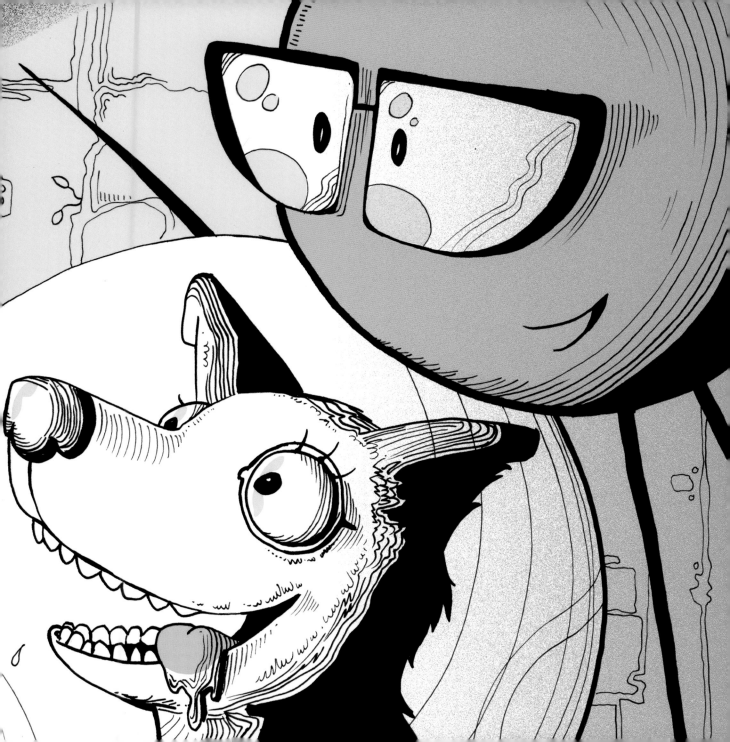

But there was no response,
only silence.

But he didn't really care—he loved exploring no matter what. So, Curiosity, the robot rover, played with Sputnik, the forgotten spaceship, and Laika, the forgotten space-dog.

As his radio battery ran out, Curiosity
sighed a happy sigh. He'd done it.
Earth would never know,
but there was life on Mars.

AUTHOR'S NOTE

The curious robot rover is not just a figment of our imaginations. On August 6, 2012, after a voyage of 253 days, NASA's *Curiosity* rover landed on Mars. The largest and most advanced robot rover ever to land on Mars, part of *Curiosity's* mission is to look for signs of life on the planet. While the life probably won't be in the form of Laika (the first dog in space) or Sputnik (the first satellite in space), if *Curiosity* finds evidence of even the smallest, single-celled forms of life, it would be one of the most significant discoveries in history. Mission control would definitely want to know.

At the time of publication of this book, its mission is ongoing and due to last another year. You can find out more here:

http://www.nasa.gov/mission_pages/msl/index.html

Sky Pony Press books may be purchased in bulk at special discounts for sales promotion, corporate gifts, fund-raising, or educational purposes. Special editions can also be created to specifications. For details, contact the Special Sales Department, Sky Pony Press, 307 West 36th Street, 11th Floor, New York, NY 10018 or info@skyhorsepublishing.com.

Sky Pony® is a registered trademark of Skyhorse Publishing, Inc.®, a Delaware corporation.

Visit our website at www.skyponypress.com.

10 9 8 7 6 5 4 3 2 1

Manufactured in China, June 2013
This product conforms to CPSIA 2008

Library of Congress Cataloging-in-Publication Data is available on file.
ISBN: 978-1-62087-994-8